OLIVE & ROGER

HOMER

DAZZLE

BANJO

MARCO POLO

LILYANNA

PIPER

Book Buddies

Ivy Lost and Found

Cynthia Lord

illustrated by

Stephanie Graegin

CANDLEWICK PRESS

Text copyright © 2021 by Cynthia Lord
Illustrations copyright © 2021 by Stephanie Graegin

First edition 2021

Library of Congress Catalog Card Number pending
ISBN 978-1-5362-1354-6

21 22 23 24 25 26 LBM 10 9 8 7 6 5 4 3 2 1

Printed in Melrose Park, IL, USA

This book was typeset in Sabon.
The illustrations were created digitally.

Candlewick Press
99 Dover Street
Somerville, Massachusetts 02144

www.candlewick.com

To Julia

CL

For my nieces

SG

CHAPTER ONE

Ivy

Ivy's first memory was the birthday party. There was music and bright balloons. A girl's face lit up with joy.

"A doll!" Anne had cried. She cut the strings and untwisted the ties that held Ivy in her store box. "I'll name you Ivy," Anne whispered into Ivy's dark braids.

After that, it was always the two of them: Ivy and Anne.

On warm summer days, Anne played with Ivy outside in the garden. Ivy's tiny blue boots left footprints in the mud.

On gray, rainy afternoons, Anne made new clothes for Ivy. She stitched soft dresses and pants

from scraps of fabric and lace. She made belts from string and rubber bands. She knit sweaters from leftover bits of yarn. Ivy loved them all.

On icy winter nights, snow fell outside the windows. Anne tucked Ivy into blankets and read fairy tales to her. Ivy's favorite part was always "happily ever after."

And every night before she fell asleep, Anne whispered her most secret worries and hopes to Ivy. Ivy always listened.

She never imagined it could change.

As Anne grew up, trips to the garden stopped. Ivy's tiny blue boots stayed clean.

She wore the same white pants and gray sweater for years.

On icy winter nights, Ivy stayed on the shelf. She watched snow fall outside the window while Anne slept.

Missing someone hurts, Ivy thought. *This is how it feels to be forgotten.*

Then one day Ivy was brought to the attic. She was placed in a box with some old clothes.

Ivy went to sleep. Memories came and went, like dreams. Over and over, Ivy remembered the birthday party, the trips to the garden, new clothes, and icy nights, tucked in blankets.

Until one day . . .

The box opened again.

Anne's eyes were older now, but they lit up with joy.

"Ivy!" she cried. "I remember you."

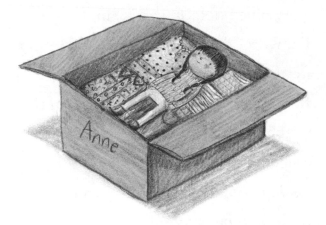

CHAPTER TWO

The Library

Ivy peeked out of Anne's tote bag. Everything was very bright after the dark box. There was so much to see!

There were books on long shelves, in bins, and on bookcases. Shiny posters were on the walls. There was even a shelf of stuffed animals and toys with a sign: BOOK BUDDIES.

Ivy had never seen so many children. Some played games. Some did puzzles at little tables. Others sat in beanbags, listening to their parents read.

"Welcome to the library," Anne called to everyone. "Story time will start in five minutes. Today I'm reading books about bears. Get ready to growl!"

Anne carried Ivy to the Book Buddies shelf. A little girl with pigtails and overalls was patting the toy unicorn's tail.

"Hi, Sophie!" Anne said to the girl. "I have a surprise. I helped my mom clean out her attic yesterday, and look who I found!" She took Ivy from the tote bag. "It's my old doll, Ivy."

Old doll? Ivy's heart broke.

"Today she'll join the Book Buddies," Anne said. "Children can borrow her and read stories to her, like I did."

Ivy didn't want to be borrowed. She wanted to belong to Anne. She wanted to be her favorite toy again.

Sophie smiled. "She can meet the other Book Buddies."

"That's a great idea!" Anne turned Ivy toward a brown bear with a black nose. "Ivy, this is Banjo." Next was a fluffy black-and-white hen with her yellow chick. "Here are Olive and little Roger."

Banjo and Olive looked sweet. Roger had mischief in his eyes. Ivy liked them all.

Homer the owl had brown feathers, fierce yellow eyes, and white tufts on his head. Ivy tried to smile bravely.

"And here's Dazzle!" Sophie pointed to a snow-white unicorn with a sparkly pink tail. "Dazzle is a *boy*," she told Ivy. "He likes stories with magic."

Piper was a gray-and-white flying squirrel. Next to him was a tiny mouse wearing a wool vest and an acorn-cap hat. "That's Marco Polo," Anne said. "He likes to explore."

"And this is Lilyanna. She's my favorite!" Sophie said.

9

Lilyanna was another doll. She had a gold crown and long sunshine-colored hair. She wore a glittery purple dress with laces up the front.

A princess! Just like in the fairy tales.

"They can be friends," Anne said. "Lilyanna will love having another library doll."

Ivy thought she heard Lilyanna give a tiny sniff, like that wasn't true.

Ivy had always loved her own black braids, little garden boots, homemade pants, and gray sweater. But next to Lilyanna, she felt plain and not even a little bit glittery.

Anne set Ivy gently on the shelf between the hen and the unicorn.

"Come on, Banjo!" Anne picked up the brown bear. "You're the guest of honor at story time today. Our first book is *Brown Bear, Brown Bear, What Do You See?*"

Anne carried Banjo over her shoulder. He smiled back at the other toys.

Ivy wished she could hear the stories, too. Maybe if she closed her eyes and listened really hard . . .

"Are they gone?" a deep voice asked.

CHAPTER THREE

The Toys

The unicorn stretched. "My legs hurt. I've been sitting still for so long," he said in his deep voice.

"I wish Anne would do another *princess* story time," Lilyanna whined. "The last one was at the Valentine's tea party. Anne put me on a special chair. She read fairy tales—"

"Yes, dear. You've told us many times," the hen clucked. "Where are our manners? We have someone new!" Olive put her soft wing around Ivy.

Ivy smiled shyly at Olive. Maybe she could make a friend? Someone to help her understand this new place? Ivy had never had a friend before, except for Anne.

"Whooo are you?" Homer hooted. "What's your story?"

"My story?" Ivy asked.

Piper nodded. "Every toy has a story. I came from a yard sale. Before that, I used to fly through the trees."

"Only when your child threw you," Homer said. "Flying squirrels don't really fly. Not like owls. We fly up. Flying squirrels only fly *down*!"

"I *did* fly," Piper said quietly. "You don't know everything, Homer."

The little mouse tugged on the edge of Ivy's sweater. "I was a Christmas ornament! Anne cut off my string so I could be a real toy. She named me Marco Polo because I'm a brave explorer."

"Anne bought me new for the Valentine's tea party," Lilyanna said. "I'm not an old ornament or a hand-me-down toy."

"Shh," Dazzle said. "I want to hear Ivy's story."

Lilyanna sniffed.

"I was Anne's toy when she was young." Ivy didn't say *favorite toy* because she didn't want to hurt anyone's feelings.

"You must be very old!" Roger peeped.

"Roger, it's not polite to call another toy old," Olive scolded her chick. "Better to say 'well loved.'"

"Tell us about Anne as a child," Dazzle said. "She's always been a grown-up to us."

"I was her birthday present," Ivy began. Then she told them about the clothes Anne had made. She described the trips to the garden. She even told them about the stories Anne had read aloud on icy winter nights, tucked in blankets.

Ivy didn't tell them about being forgotten. It was too sad to remember that. "But that's over now," she said simply.

"Maybe not," Homer said. "I've been tucked in blankets with lots of children since I became a Book Buddy."

Olive nodded. "We're borrowed for two weeks at a time. Roger and I always go together."

"Children play with us and read us stories," Dazzle said.

"I've been to Mexico," Lilyanna bragged. "The family took me on *vacation* with them. I went to the beach and in a hot tub."

"I fell in the toilet once!" Roger said proudly. "The mother dried me with a hair dryer!"

"It was terrifying!" Olive clucked. "Thank goodness the toilet was *clean*!"

"Every borrowing is a new adventure," Piper said. "We each have a journal. The child can draw or write what we did at their house. So our stories keep going and going."

Ivy tried to smile. Borrowing did sound better than being forgotten. It didn't sound as good as belonging to your own child, though.

Maybe these toys had never been loved like that? *Once you've truly belonged, nothing else comes close,* Ivy thought.

"I hope I'm not borrowed by a baby this time," Dazzle said. "The last baby drooled on me. Thank goodness I'm machine washable."

"I hope my next family doesn't have a cat," Marco Polo said. "I was almost swallowed last time!"

"I know Sophie will pick me," Lilyanna said. "I'm her favorite. She said so."

Homer's ears twitched. "Shh, everyone! I hear the children coming. Get back to your places."

"Roger, fluff your fluff!" Olive said. "We want a child to pick us!"

Ivy did not want to be picked. She leaned closer to Dazzle, hoping his big tail would hide her. She wanted to stay at the library. Then Anne would see her every day and remember how much she loved her.

Children came rushing into the room. Ivy peeked out from Dazzle's tail. *Don't pick me,* she wished.

Sophie stopped at the toy shelf with a little boy and an older girl. The little boy grabbed the flying squirrel. "Piper!"

Sophie picked up the princess. "I want to borrow Lilyanna again!" She turned to the older girl beside her. "And look, Fern! A new doll. We can pretend our dolls are sisters. Just like us!"

Ivy heard Lilyanna give a tiny sniff at the word *sisters*.

Fern shook her head. "I don't play with dolls, Sophie."

Whew! Ivy thought. *That was a close call.*

Other children came to the toy shelf. Ivy peeked between the strands of Dazzle's tail. She saw Homer being hugged by a girl. A boy was helping Marco Polo climb the puzzle boxes. Then a girl picked up Dazzle and tucked him under her arm.

Ivy had nowhere to hide.

"Quick!" Sophie grabbed Ivy. "Take her, Fern. Before someone else borrows her!"

Ivy looked into Fern's eyes. *She doesn't want me,* Ivy thought.

"Come on! We have to check out," Sophie said.

Fern sighed and took Ivy.

Ivy was borrowed.

CHAPTER FOUR

Fern

Fern loved both her mom and her dad, but it was hard living in two houses.

At Mom's house, Fern was an only child. She had her own bedroom. She could put her things where she wanted. No one ever took them or moved them. At night her dog, Dusty, slept on the floor beside her bed.

Dad's house was louder and more crowded. After the divorce, Dad had married a woman named Nicole, who already had two children. Sophie was six years old and Ethan was four. Dad lived too far away for Fern to visit every week. So most weeks, Fern talked to Dad on the phone and sent him drawings and photos. But during school vacations and for two weeks in the summer, she came to Dad's house to stay.

When Fern lived with Dad, she shared a room with Sophie. The room was full of Sophie's things. The bottom dresser drawer was supposed to be left empty for Fern. But when Fern opened the drawer to put her things away, it was never empty. There were always notes and drawings from Sophie.

Fern knew that Sophie was trying to be nice, so it didn't feel right to complain. It bothered her, though. Nothing at Dad's was just hers. Not even her drawer.

Fern had to go everywhere with Sophie and Ethan, too. She didn't want to go to the library that morning. Story time was for younger kids, she said. Not for eight-year-olds.

Nicole said she couldn't stay home alone.

So Fern sat in the back with the parents. While Anne read bear stories and the kids sang songs, Fern looked at a library book about fairy houses. It showed how to make them from natural things like sticks, pine cones, rocks, and leaves.

It looked like fun! There were woods around Dad's house. A perfect place to build a fairy house. If she went outdoors quietly, she might escape Sophie and Ethan for a little while, too.

"Can I take this book home?" she whispered to Nicole.

Nicole smiled. "Sure!"

Fern didn't want to borrow a doll, though. She didn't even really like dolls. But when Sophie wanted something, it was hard to say no.

"Fern and I are going to play dolls!" Sophie told Anne as they checked out their toys and books. "I've been waiting for her to come for *weeks*!"

Anne smiled at Fern. "You'll be the first child to borrow Ivy." She scanned the bar code on the fairy-house book and Ivy's small journal. "And I bet Ivy would love a fairy house! She always did like to go outside."

"That's a great idea!" Sophie said. "We can make fairy houses for our dolls. There are lots of sticks and pine cones in the woods."

"How fun!" Anne said. "I'm excited to read about their adventures in their journals."

Fern held the fairy-house book tightly. *I'll wait until Sophie and Ethan are busy*, she thought. *Then I'll sneak outside to build my fairy house by myself.*

"I'm going to make Lilyanna a campsite!" Sophie said as they walked out the door.

CHAPTER FIVE

Outdoors

Ivy hadn't been outside to play in a long time. The sun warmed her hair. The breeze tickled her hands. The pine needles were a soft, sweet-smelling pillow to sit on.

Next to her, Fern had gathered bits of bark, sticks, pine cones, small stones, and other natural things. "The fairy-house book says never use anything that's still growing," she said out loud.

Is Fern talking to me? Ivy wondered. But Fern had said she didn't play with dolls.

For the base of the house, Fern had chosen an oak tree with space between its roots. She added long pine cones to make walls. Pine branches across the top made a roof.

She put Ivy inside.

It smelled like Christmas. Ivy leaned back, remembering. Anne had always wrapped a little Christmas present, just for her. One year Anne knit Ivy a scarf. Another Christmas there was a tea set with tiny plates and cups. The next year there was a small dresser for Ivy's clothes.

"I have a dog named Dusty at my other house," Fern said quietly. "I wish he could come to Dad's house with me, but his fur makes Sophie sneeze."

Fern *was* talking to her! Ivy saw tears in Fern's eyes.

"It's not that I don't like Sophie," Fern said. "She's never mean to me, but I have to share everything with her. It's okay to share the room, but I wish I could have Dad to myself, even just for a few minutes. Sophie gets to have him all the time."

Fern is missing someone, too. Ivy's heart hurt. She wanted to help Fern, but she didn't know how.

"I miss Dusty," Fern said, making a pathway to the fairy house with small stones. "He's a good listener."

I can listen, Ivy thought.

"I don't usually play with dolls," Fern said, "but I like you because—"

Suddenly, a voice rang out. "There you are, Fern! We've been looking for you!"

It was Sophie and Ethan. Fern wiped her eyes quickly.

"You didn't tell us it was time to make the fairy houses!" Sophie said. "I'm going to build

Lilyanna's campsite right next to you! Then our dolls can visit!" She sat Lilyanna on the rock pathway to Fern's fairy house.

"Piper can fly into the trees!" Ethan threw the squirrel high. Piper swished between branches and past leaves. A few acorns fell to the ground.

"Piper is getting food for everyone!" Ethan said happily. He caught Piper coming down. Then Ethan threw Piper even higher into the oak tree.

More acorns fell. This time, Piper didn't come down with them.

"Oh no!" Ethan cried. "He's stuck on a branch!"

"Don't worry," Sophie said. "We can get him down. Just throw something else at him. It will knock him loose."

"Ivy can rescue him!" Ethan grabbed Ivy from the fairy house, bumping the branches off the roof. Pine cones rolled off the walls. He aimed Ivy at the branches.

"Ethan, stop!" Fern cried.

It was too late.

Ivy felt herself soaring upward. Leaves and branches brushed by her. She closed her eyes. *Please let someone catch me!* she wished.

She landed with a thump on something soft. She opened her eyes.

"Hi," Piper said beneath her. "We're in a tree!"

CHAPTER SIX

Forgotten

Ivy looked over Piper's shoulder and down toward the ground. She'd never been so high. If she fell from here, could she break her leg or arm?

Below her, a sparrow jumped from branch to branch. Everything on the ground looked far away and small. The children looked up, but Ivy didn't know if they could even see her between the branches.

"Why do you always have to ruin every-thing?" Fern snapped at Sophie and Ethan. She turned and ran for the house.

Sophie ran after her. Ethan followed, yelling, "I didn't mean to!"

Ivy waited for them to come back.

She waited as the sun sank low in the sky.

She waited as the bats came out of hiding and flew beneath her.

She waited as the crickets started to chirp.

In the dusk, Ivy could barely make out Lilyanna's bright yellow hair on the ground far below them.

Lilyanna would be easy to find, but what about her and Piper?

"Someone will come," Piper said. "The family only gets to borrow us for two weeks. They'll get a notice if we aren't returned on time."

Two weeks felt like forever.

Nothing could be worse than this, Ivy thought.

Then it started to rain.

As night came, Ivy rested her head on Piper's wet fur. What if no one ever came? After a while, her braids would get messy in the wind.

Her clothes would get shabby and faded. Snow would come and cover them both.

She'd never see Anne again.

"When kids throw me, I always come back down," Piper said under her. "This is the first time I've only flown *up*. Thank you for trying to save me, Ivy."

"Thank you for saving me, too," Ivy said. "I might have broken my leg or arm if I hadn't landed on you."

"Soft animals don't break. We can rip, but then someone can sew us up again." Piper sighed. "I'm glad you're here, Ivy. I feel braver with you."

Ivy felt warm inside. She'd never had a toy friend before. If they were forgotten, at least they had each other. "And I feel braver with you, Piper."

Ivy liked that being friends made them both braver. It gave her a brave idea.

"I don't know if anyone will come," Ivy said, "so let's save ourselves."

"How?" Piper asked.

"You're a flying squirrel, right?" Ivy said. "That means you can fly!"

"No," Piper said sadly. "Homer was right. I pretend I can fly, but really, I can only fly *down*."

"Don't you see?" Ivy asked, smiling. "That's perfect!"

"It is?" Piper asked.

Ivy nodded. "*Down* is where we want to go."

CHAPTER SEVEN

Down

Ivy wrapped her arms tightly around Piper's neck. "Ready? Set? Fly!"

Piper pushed off the branch. He spread his legs wide. The skin between his paws stretched to catch the air, like a parachute. "Wheee!"

Ivy kept her eyes open and held on tight. Piper swerved and turned to avoid branches and leaves.

"Wheee!" she said.

They hit the ground with a thump and a bounce.

"Are you okay?" Piper asked.

"No!" Lilyanna whined. "My hair is wet! It has sticks in it! And I'm"—she shivered—"dirty!"

"I meant *Ivy*," Piper said.

Ivy moved her arms and legs. No broken parts! "Yes, I'm okay," she said. "That was amazing!"

"Are you kidding me?" Lilyanna asked. "This is not amazing! It's night. It's raining. We've been *forgotten*." She sniffed. "It's Fern's fault!"

Ivy sniffed back at her. "It is not! Fern and I were just fine until Sophie and Ethan came outside!"

"Fern didn't even want to borrow you," Lilyanna said coldly.

Ivy paused. It was true. Fern hadn't wanted her, and Ivy hadn't wanted to be borrowed. Something had changed, though.

Ivy had liked being played with again. Fern had said, *I don't usually play with dolls, but I like you because—*

Because why?

Ivy really wanted to know.

"I'm sorry," Lilyanna said quietly. "I shouldn't have said that. I've never been forgotten before."

"I have," Ivy said.

Piper and Lilyanna both gasped.

Ivy nodded. "I was forgotten in a box for a very long time. It *was* lonely and sad, but—"

Piper and Lilyanna looked surprised.

But? Ivy couldn't believe she'd said that word, either. Wasn't being forgotten the worst thing that could ever happen?

Being forgotten had been lonely and sad, *but*—

Ivy had made new friends.

A child had played with her again.

She'd had a brave adventure.

She smiled. "Being forgotten means you can be found again."

CHAPTER EIGHT

Found

Overnight the rain stopped. The stars came out. Then Ivy watched the sunrise, pink and gold. It was the most beautiful thing she'd ever seen.

She listened to the birds singing and the squirrels chattering.

She heard the leaves swish high above her in the trees. Ivy closed her eyes and remembered the view from up there.

"I spent the whole night outside, like a real flying squirrel!" Piper said proudly. "We're nighttime animals, you know."

Ivy opened her eyes. "And I saw the world from up in a tree. I'll never forget it!"

They both looked at Lilyanna.

She shrugged. "I got dirty for the first time."

"Really?" Ivy asked, surprised. "Hasn't a child ever played with you in a garden?"

Lilyanna shook her head. "Never."

Ivy felt sorry for her. "Dirt is only on the outside. It doesn't change who you are on the inside," she said. "My boots have been muddy many times. Anne always cleaned them with a wet washcloth."

"I can go in the washing machine. It says so on my tag." Piper showed them. "Machine washable! Then I go around and around in the dryer. It's warm and toasty in there. When I'm done, I'm fluffy and smell sweet."

"Shh!" Lilyanna said. "Someone's coming!"

Then Ivy heard the footsteps, too. It was Fern! Dad walked beside her carrying a big ladder.

"Ivy and Piper! Here they are! How did they get out of the tree?" Fern picked up Ivy. She moved Ivy's arms and legs. "Thank goodness she's not broken!"

"The wind must've blown them down." Dad set the ladder on the ground. "And what's this?"

They both looked at Lilyanna sitting among the scattered pine cones and pine branches that had been Fern's fairy house. Only the stone path was left.

"I just wanted to make a fairy house for Ivy," Fern said. "But Sophie had to make Lilyanna a campsite right next to me, and Ethan threw Piper into the tree. Why do they have to ruin everything? If they had let me play by myself, this wouldn't have happened."

"I know," Dad said. "Sophie and Ethan are just excited that you're here."

"But when we play together, they take over. It's not fair that I have to share everything all the time." Fern looked up at Dad. "The hardest part is sharing *you*. Sophie and Ethan get you every day. I only get you on vacations."

Dad put his arm around Fern. "I'm sorry, honey."

"I miss you," she said, leaning against him.

"I miss you, too," Dad said. "I miss you every day that we're apart. I can see that we need to make a few changes, though. I want you to be happy here."

Fern hugged Dad and he hugged her back.

"I'm glad to know how you feel," Dad said. "Let's think of new ideas to make things better, okay?"

"Okay." Fern saw a movement in the trees. Sophie and Ethan were peeking around a tree trunk. They were trying to hide, but the tree was too small and they were easy to see. Fern giggled because they looked so funny.

"I'm sorry I yelled at you," Fern called to them.

"We just wanted to play with you," Sophie said, coming out from behind the tree.

"I do want to play with you *sometimes*," Fern said. "But other times I like to do things on my own. I'd like you to ask me first."

Sophie and Ethan both nodded.

Fern took a deep breath. It was hard to tell everyone how she felt, but it did make her feel better. "Sophie, I need some things that are only mine—like my drawer. When you put notes in there, I feel like a visitor in your room, not like I belong there."

"Oh," said Sophie. "I wanted to show you I'm happy you're here. I won't do it anymore."

Fern thought about what Dad had said about making things better. "I have a new idea," she said. "Dad, could we get a whiteboard for our room? Sophie could write messages to me there. And I could write messages to her?"

"Yes!" Sophie said.

"That's a wonderful idea," Dad said. "We'll get a whiteboard this week."

"And the fairy house isn't ruined forever,"
Fern said. "It just needs to be put back together."

"We can help with—!" Sophie stopped. She
looked down at the ground. "Can we help?"

Fern smiled. "Yes."

"I can look for some pine branches," Dad said.

"I'll get more rocks!" Ethan said.

"Lilyanna and I will help with the pine cones!" Sophie added. "She's an outdoorsy princess!"

Ivy heard Lilyanna sniff. This time it didn't sound like an unhappy sniff, though.

Ivy looked over at Lilyanna's dirty face. A few pine needles were stuck in her long hair, but her eyes glittered with happy tears.

This will be one of my best memories ever, Ivy thought.

CHAPTER NINE

Just Right

That night, Fern gave Ivy a bubble bath in the sink.

She cleaned Ivy's boots with a warm, wet washcloth.

She brushed and braided Ivy's hair.

Nicole helped Fern use her sewing machine. Together they made a nightgown for Ivy to wear while her sweater and pants were in the washing machine and dryer (with Piper!).

Then Fern tucked Ivy into blankets beside her. Across the room, Sophie tucked Lilyanna into bed with her, too.

Fern opened a book. "Once upon a time," she read aloud, "there was a girl named Cinderella."

As Fern read, Ivy imagined the whole story. She didn't hear Lilyanna sniff once. Not even when Cinderella was dirty from cleaning the fireplace ashes.

Dirt is only on the outside, Ivy thought.

In the middle of the story, Dad came in and listened, too. He waited in the doorway until Fern finished. "And they lived happily ever after."

Then he came in and kissed Sophie and Fern on their foreheads. "Good night, sweethearts. Nicole and I thought we'd all go to the beach tomorrow. Would you like that?"

"Yes!" Sophie said.

Fern nodded. "Can Ivy come, too?"

"Of course." Dad kissed Ivy's tiny forehead. "As long as she doesn't climb any more trees!"

"Ivy does like adventures." Fern laid her cheek on Ivy's head.

Dad smiled. "Fern, I have a new idea. At the beach tomorrow, let's take a little walk together, just you and me."

Fern grinned. "That would be fun."

After Dad turned out the light, Fern said good night to Sophie. "Do you want to bring some buckets tomorrow? We could build a sandcastle for Lilyanna."

"And Ivy!" Sophie said.

Snuggled next to Fern, Ivy remembered. This time, she didn't start with Anne's birthday party.

She remembered the fairy house.

She remembered the view from up in the tree and flying down with Piper.

She remembered a warm bubble bath and listening to a story tucked in blankets with Fern.

Maybe borrowing isn't so bad after all, she thought.

In fact, maybe borrowing was just right.

CHAPTER TEN

Happily Ever After

At the end of two weeks, it was time for Fern to go home to Mom's house. She wanted to see Mom and Dusty, but she knew she'd miss Dad, Nicole, Ethan, Sophie, and Ivy.

It was time for Ivy to go home, too.

At the library, Ethan showed Anne the drawings he'd made in Piper's journal. Piper was flying up and down through the trees. "He was a real flying squirrel!"

"Lilyanna went to the beach!" Sophie showed Anne her drawing of Lilyanna building a sandcastle with Piper and Ivy. "Lilyanna's an outdoorsy princess."

Fern opened Ivy's journal to the first page. "Once upon a time, there was a doll named Ivy," she read aloud. There were stories and pictures of Ivy in the fairy house. Ivy at the beach. Ivy going down the slide at the playground. Ivy climbing the garden vines and listening to Fern read stories. Fern had filled up four pages!

Ivy
Once upon a time, there was a doll named Ivy.

Ivy has a fairy house.

"Nicole and I made Ivy a nightgown," Fern said. "I left it in my drawer for Ivy to wear the next time I'm home at Dad's."

Next time! Ivy liked those words.

"Let me know when you're coming," Anne said. "I'll reserve her for you."

Fern gave Ivy one last hug. "I never much played with dolls, but I like you," she whispered into Ivy's ear, "because you're a good listener and a great friend."

Ivy's heart was full. She didn't even mind being put on the Book Buddies shelf. She was glad to see her toy friends again.

"Story time!" Anne called to the families in the library. "Today I have a surprise. I'm reading books about gardens, and I have a new toy for the Book Buddies shelf. He'll be our special guest today."

A new toy? Everyone tried to peek as Anne pulled something from her tote bag.

Ivy saw a long white beard and a tall, pointy purple hat. "I couldn't resist him!" Anne said. "He's Nugget the garden gnome!"

Ivy smiled as Anne led the families off to story time. She wasn't the new toy anymore. It would be fun to tell Nugget about being borrowed. It might be scary or hard at first, but it was wonderful in the end.

"Are they gone?" Dazzle asked, stretching his legs.

"I had a great borrowing," Marco Polo said. "I drove a toy car and slept in a dollhouse."

"A dog grabbed me," Roger said. "He took me outside!"

"My heart almost exploded with worry!" Olive clucked. "Thank goodness the child found Roger just in time. He was nearly buried!"

Roger nodded. "It was great!"

"I got dirty," Lilyanna said. "Did you know dirt is only on the outside? Mud and sand wash off."

"Ivy and I got stuck in a tree. I rescued us by flying down." Piper smiled proudly at Homer. "Because *down* was where we needed to go."

"And we were forgotten," Lilyanna added quietly.

The other toys gasped.

"Oh my!" Olive covered Roger's ears with her wings. "A toy's worst nightmare!"

"It was awful," Lilyanna agreed. "But then Ivy said being forgotten means you can be found again."

"And we were!" Piper said.

"Wow," Banjo said. "What an adventure!"

Homer nodded. "What did you think of your first borrowing, Ivy?"

Ivy thought for a moment. It *had* been an adventure. Some parts had been hard, but most parts were wonderful.

She didn't know where to begin. So she started at the end. "I think that . . ."

The toys all leaned close to hear.

She grinned. "I can't wait to be borrowed again!"

When story time was over, Ivy didn't hide behind Dazzle's tail. She sat up straight so the children would see her. She wanted them to know that she was a good listener and a great friend. She was not afraid to get her boots dirty. She wanted to be borrowed.

There were lots of empty pages still in her journal—plenty of room for more adventures with other kids. Kids who needed a special friend to play with and read to and listen to them.

Then after each borrowing, she'd come back to Anne and her Book Buddy friends at the library. Over and over.

Happily ever after.

1.

Once upon a time there was an eighteen-year-old girl who dragged her butt out of bed and hauled it all the way to school on a sunny day in May.

2.

That was me.

3.

Normal kids (like me) thought high school was cool for the first three days in ninth grade. Then it became a big yawn, the kind of yawn that showed the fillings in your teeth and the white stuff on your tongue you didn't scrape off with your toothbrush.

Sometimes I wondered why I bothered. Normal kids (me again), we weren't going to college, no matter what anybody said. I could read and write and add and do nails and fix hair

For Scot,
because every dance is his

VIKING
Published by Penguin Group
Penguin Young Readers Group, 345 Hudson Street, New York, New York 10014, U.S.A.
Penguin Group (Canada), 10 Alcorn Avenue, Toronto, Ontario, Canada M4V 3B2
(a division of Pearson Penguin Canada Inc.)
Penguin Books Ltd, 80 Strand, London WC2R 0RL, England
Penguin Ireland, 25 St Stephen's Green, Dublin 2, Ireland
(a division of Penguin Books Ltd)
Penguin Group (Australia), 250 Camberwell Road, Camberwell, Victoria 3124, Australia
(a division of Pearson Australia Group Pty Ltd)
Penguin Books India Pvt Ltd, 11 Community Centre, Panchsheel Park,
New Delhi - 110 017, India
Penguin Group (NZ), Cnr Airborne and Rosedale Roads, Albany, Auckland, New Zealand
(a division of Pearson New Zealand Ltd)
Penguin Books (South Africa) (Pty) Ltd, 24 Sturdee Avenue, Rosebank,
Johannesburg 2196, South Africa

Penguin Books Ltd, Registered Offices: 80 Strand, London WC2R 0RL, England

First published in 2005 by Viking, a division of Penguin Young Readers Group

1 3 5 7 9 10 8 6 4 2

LIBRARY OF CONGRESS CATALOGING-IN-PUBLICATION DATA
Anderson, Laurie Halse.
Prom / Laurie Halse Anderson.
p. cm.
Summary: Eighteen-year-old Ash wants nothing to do with senior prom,
but when disaster strikes and her desperate friend, Nat, needs her help to get it
back on track, Ash's involvement transforms her life.
ISBN 0-670-05974-9 (hardcover)
[1. Proms—Fiction. 2. High schools—Fiction. 3. Schools—Fiction. 4. Self-realization—
Fiction. 5. Family life—Pennsylvania—Fiction. 6. Pennsylvania—Fiction.] I. Title.
PZ7.A54385Pr 2005
[Fic]—dc22
2004014974

Printed in U.S.A.
Set in Berkeley

140.

Ma was hanging up the phone when we walked back in.

"Anything?" she asked.

"Nothing," I said. "You?"

"No one's seen her. Your aunts are still looking. I'm gonna call the cops."

"She's been missing for fifteen minutes. Cops won't get involved until she's gone for twenty-four hours," Dad said.

"That's for normal people," I said. "They'll search right away if it's a crazy old lady."

"Especially if you tell them she can bake," TJ said, licking the sugar off his fingers.

"I think we should tell Yevgeny and Natalia," Ma said.

"You're overreacting, Mary Alice," Dad said. "This ain't good for you. Just relax, okay? She'll be back before you know it."

"What is wrong with you?" Ma yelled. "That poor woman is out there alone and lonely—"

"Hold it!" I stepped in between them. "I know where she is. Grab the condoms and get in the car."

"The old lady needs condoms?" Dad asked.

141.

Two minutes later, we were headed for my school in the white Caddy. Ma rode shotgun. I was stuffed in back like a forgotten piece of pink Kleenex.

"This is a real hot date," TJ muttered.

"Don't be an ass," I said.

"What is it with you?" he asked. "First you love me, then you hate me, get a tux, take the tux back. Now we're tracking down the old kook. . . . "

I flicked the back of his head with my fingers. "Shut up and drive."

"Hey," he yelled. "I'm just saying."

"Don't yell at my kid." Ma slapped him upside the head. "And step on it."

142.

As we pulled into the school driveway, TJ had to slow the Caddy to a crawl.

"Damn," he said.

"Yeah," I said.

Stick enough limos in a parking lot, and even Carceras can look classy. Crowds of parents and friends lined the sidewalk that led up to the front door. The dressed-up, glammed-out prom couples strolled down the sidewalk, smiling for the cameras and waving to their fans. It was our very own red carpet show.

"Are you sure she's here?" TJ asked.

"Pull over." I grabbed the cardboard box. "We'll get out. You park and meet us at the door."

I got out first and helped Ma. That baby of hers was getting bigger by the minute. We caught some confused looks as she took my arm and we got in the line of couples waiting to get in. Not many girls take their pregnant mothers to the prom, I guess. Not many show up in their slippers, either.

As we got closer to the door, a few kids recognized me.

"Ashley!"

"Shake it, *mami*!"

"Whoa, girl!"

"Looking good, Hannigan."

Ma pulled my arm closer. "Let's cut to the front of the line."

"We can't. It's too crowded. And don't you dare pull the 'baby's coming' routine again. Nobody will care, trust me. They're here for fun."

The line inched forward. Ma and I scanned the crowd, but there was no sign of Grandma. I knew she was here, knew it in my bones. All of this was coming together in a weird way, like when it was done, it was going to make sense, but we weren't quite there yet.

A minute later, TJ joined us. "Yo, Ash. We got a problem."

"We got a lot of them."

"I heard that Gilroy is checking tickets at the door. With school security and a cop." He held me back. "We can't let him see me."

"What are you talking about? You dropped out last year. He can't do anything to you now."

TJ ran his hands through his hair, keeping his eyes on the door. "Gilroy said he'd press charges if I ever showed my face again."

Ma was pretending not to listen, but she was catching every word.

"Wait a minute," I said. "We were going to come here,

before I got busted. To the prom. How were you gonna get past Gilroy then?"

TJ wiped the hair gel that stuck to his hands on his pants. "I was going to pay a buddy to open a bathroom window so I could sneak in."

"Very sophisticated," Ma muttered.

TJ stepped closer and whispered in my ear. "Come on, babe. Your mother can talk to Gilroy, explain about old Grandma. We'll wait back here, hang by the wall, check everybody out."

The line ahead of us moved and the line behind us pushed. I took a few steps forward with Ma. TJ came, too, his eyes on the door.

"I need to go inside," I said. "I'm sure she's there. She's batty about this whole prom thing, just like Nat. Look at the dress she made, for crying out loud."

"Just explain who you're looking for to the security guards," TJ said. His voice was tight.

I held the box up. "I want to sneak these in, too. The security guards won't like that."

TJ wrapped his arms around me and blew gently in my ear. "Let 'em get their own damn protection. You and me have better plans for that box. Come on, babe."

"Let go of me," I said.

TJ squeezed tighter. "You don't want to be a part of this shit." He nibbled my neck and whispered. "I want to get you out of that dress."

I peeled his arms off me and stepped away.

"Hello? Are you crazy? I do too want to be a part of this 'shit.' And I'm keeping the dress on, thank you very much."

He rolled his eyes.

"You don't like it, you can leave," I said.

"Maybe I will."

"Maybe you should."

"Maybe I'll find somebody else to take home."

"Knock yourself out, asshole." I grabbed Ma's arm. "Emergency!" I shouted. "We got an emergency here!"

Ma and me butted and barged our way to the front of the line. TJ fell back into the shadows.

"About time you told him where to get off," Ma said.

143.

The security guards stood in our way.

"We're looking for an old lady," I said. "I know she's here."

"We don't got old ladies here," the first guard said, eyeing my mother. "This is the prom."

"Watch it, buster," Ma said.

"What's in the box?" the second guard asked.

"Her medication," I said.

"Right. That's a good one. Go home now."

"No, listen—"

Mr. Gilroy stepped in between the two guards, a sick ferret smile on his face.

Damn.

"Miss Hannigan. I was afraid of something like this. You are determined to force a confrontation, aren't you?"

The kids behind us pushed a little, complaining about the delay.

"Mr. Gilroy, it's not what you think. Let me explain."

"Miss Hannigan, you have three seconds to get off school property or I will direct this officer to escort you. We will then press charges."

"That's it!" Ma shoved me to the side. "All right, you weasel. I've had a hard day. Shut your yap and listen."

The crowd behind us went silent. Kids at Carceras can smell a good fight for miles.

"Madam, can I help you?"

Ma bellied up to Gilroy, got right in his face and let it fly. All those years of watching Court TV were not a waste. She told him we were to look for a frail, dying Alzheimer's patient, that the police were on the way, and he was standing in the way of us saving her life.

The crowd started whispering.

Then she told him that he had been a creep when he was her Social Studies teacher back in 1988 and he was still a creep today, only now he was pathetic and twisted, too.

The crowd giggled.

Ma said that our lawyer was filing a lawsuit against Gilroy, Banks, the superintendent, and the school board for singling me out for cruel and unusual punishment. That she was going to see him fired and yank his pension. If she had her way, he'd be pumping gas by Christmas.

The crowd broke into applause. I almost did, too, but she shot me a warning look.

Now." She whipped out her extra-long Ma finger and
ook it in his face. "You are getting the hell out of our way,
and we are going inside."

Gilroy stepped to the side.

A car screeched to the curb, the driver leaning on the
horn. Everybody turned around to look.

"Oh, crap," Ma said.

It was Dad's taxicab. He leaned out the window and waved
at us. "We found her!!"

Grandma Shulmensky leaned over, waved a can of ravioli,
and blew kisses with her free hand.

"A touching family reunion," Gilroy said. "Anything else
you'd like to say, Mrs. Hannigan?"

144.

That's when we should have left. Grandma was safe. We'd
explain everything to Nat and her dad. If we were lucky, we'd
figure out a way not to get sued by Gilroy for public humilia-
tion and slander. I'd kiss and apologize at every red light and
do other things with TJ to get him to forgive me. We still had
the Caddy and I still looked fine. We could drive east to
Atlantic City and sit on the beach until the sun came up, me
still wearing my beautiful, strange gown.

Conversation started up again and the music in the gym
got loud enough for us to hear at the door. The show was
over; folks wanted in. The crowd behind us pushed forward,
and the security guard started checking their tickets and letting
them step around us and pass through the metal detectors.

The old Ashley, the normal me, would have walked a Well, limped away, listening to Ma complain, helping her in the car, putting up with TJ sticking his tongue down my throat while my parents argued, and keeping Grandma out of trouble.

"Are you okay?" Ma asked. "You look kinda funny. Your stomach acting up? I'll make you toast when we get home.'"

145.

Once upon a time there was a girl who decided to make it happen.

146.

"I'm going in," I said.

"What?" Ma squinted and leaned forward. "What did you say?"

"I'm going in. I want to dance with my friends."

"What about TJ?"

"TJ who?"

She stared for second. The crowd pushed forward again and blocked Gilroy's view of us.

"You can't go in there," Ma hissed. "Gilroy wants to arrest you. Me, too, probably."

"Seriously, Ma, I'm going in."

She pried my right eyelid all the way open and stared at my eyeball. "Are you high? Dammit, Ashley, if you got high with TJ, so help me God—"

I stroked her cheek once and put my finger on her lips.

"Straight as an arrow, Ma, listen. You always wanted to see me at the prom, right?"

"Been dreaming about it since you were born."

"Here's your chance. Plus, you get to use your acting skills in front of a huge audience. I need a distraction. You know. . . . " I waved at her belly.

She put her hands on her back and stretched a little. "You really want me to do this? You won't be embarrassed?"

"I didn't say that. Just make a distraction."

She sighed. "Lord knows I'm good at that. All right. Work your way over there to the left and hide the box of you-know-whats. The things we do for our children, I swear. . . . "

I kissed her forehead. "Thanks, Ma. You're the best."

She let out a groan. Then a louder groan. She clutched the guy in a hipster tux next to her. He backed off like she had smallpox, but Big Mike Whelan (looking very sharp in a bow tie) stepped forward and caught Ma as she fell towards him. Ma turned the groan up to a wail.

"The baby's coming!"

I let the security guards and Gilroy rush by me, then slipped behind a group of girls wearing saris. I turned around just before I snuck in the door. Ma had Gilroy in a hammerlock and was shrieking in his ear.

"The head! Mother Mary, have mercy! I can feel the head!"

She winked at me and I took off.

Hollywood lost a great one when my ma decided to drive a bus.

147.

No way. That is not the gym. Not our gym.

It was a miracle; Nat's crazy pink notebook come to life. The bleachers, the basketball nets, the BEHAVIOR AND CONSEQUENCES poster—they had disappeared in the dark. The sky was filled with twinkling white stars, the walls covered with waves of purple and silver. There were rows of round tables (with white tablecloths!) and chairs to my right and to my left. The refreshment tables were along the back wall, with the English teachers, stars in their eyes, standing behind it. And in the spotlight at the center of the gym was the dance floor, with speakers at the corners and the DJ cuing up music at the back.

I looked behind me. No guards. No Gilroy.

I picked up my skirts and mingled with the crowd.

Nat must have rented a couple hundred out-of-work celebrities, because none of the people sitting, walking, leaning over to fix a corsage, flirting, smiling, sipping orange soda out of a plastic cup—none of those people looked like they went to school with me. They were dreams in suits and tuxedos, visions in silk and chiffon and lace. Skin glowed in the light from the candles and the stars, teeth sparkled, rhinestones turned into diamonds, and everybody was in love.

Monica was the first person to see me.

"You're here!" she screamed. "You're here! I got down to one thirty-nine and my dress fits! I'm so happy. Isn't this awesome?"

"Look at you," I said. Monica, who normally wore her shorts too short, shirts too tight, and earrings ghetto-big was

gorgeous in a peach-colored gown that clung to her best assets—boobs and waist—and skimmed over the rest like it didn't matter. Her hair was long and curly. I had never seen it out of a ponytail before.

"You like it?" she asked.

"You're rocking the whole house in that thing," I said.

She grinned and nodded. "Yeah, I know." She touched her pearl earrings. "These were my mom's."

I swallowed hard, blinked away my tears and gave her another hug. "Gorgeous."

"Okay, that's enough," she said, fanning her face. "I had to put on fresh mascara two times already. Damn earrings always make me cry. Come on!"

She grabbed my hand and dragged me through the crowd to a table in the back corner. The entire prom comm was there looking like beautiful flowers, the kind you see in expensive vases in hotel lobbies. When they saw me, there was screaming, hugging, jumping up and down, and a final round of screaming. I looked around, worried that Gilroy and his goons were going to notice the commotion and drag me away, but groups of girls were doing the exact same thing all over the gym while their dates stood back and watched.

"Look at that dress!" Lauren said.

"Where did you get it?" Junie asked.

Aisha tilted her head like she was doing mental math. "Where did you get the money for it?"

I explained that a neighbor sewed it for me. My cheeks hurt from grinning so much.

When they got done staring at me, they took turns showing off. I barely recognized any of them.

Lauren's dress looked like a layer of gold skin poured over her. Aisha had on a short gray dress that sparkled in a million directions every time she moved. Junie had on an old-school prom gown: light blue satin, fitted bodice with spaghetti straps and a floor-length skirt plumped up by thick layers of netting. Lauren's hair was pulled back in a sleek bun, Aisha's was braided with thin silver ribbon, and Junie's was crimped and oiled. I checked Junie's left hand but she wasn't sporting a diamond so I didn't say anything about Charles.

The DJ started playing background music, not fast or loud enough to dance to. Around the gym, heads started bobbing, hips swaying back and forth.

"Here comes Nat!" shouted Junie.

Mr. Shulmensky rolled Nattie over to us. The whole screaming, hugging, jumping thing happened again, except that Nat couldn't jump; she could only hop on her butt in her wheelchair. Mr. S. joined the English teachers at the cake table. Nattie's eyes looked a little crossed. For sure she took that second pain pill.

We pushed Nat to the closest table and all sat down. I put the cardboard box under my chair. They fired a million questions at me about my dress and my foot (the slippers did stick out a little), and how I got in.

Finally Monica looked around and asked, "Where's TJ?"

I shrugged. "I don't know and I don't care."

Nat pumped her fist in the air. "Yes! She sees the light— woo-hoo!"

The DJ grabbed the mike.

"Are you ready to party?" he shouted.

Everybody rushed the dance floor. Charles, Ramon, and Jamel came to escort their ladies. The first beats out of the speakers were so loud they blew the hair out of my face.

A guy who looked like he could be an underwear model, with toffee-colored skin and hot fudge eyes, asked me to dance.

"She doesn't dance," Nat shouted. Monica pointed to my slippers. "She hurt her foot."

I stood up, laid my hand on the very solid arm of the mysterious, gorgeous hottie. "Oh, no, I feel great. Let's go."

I danced. I really, really danced.

148.

After playing six of my favorite songs in a row, the DJ shifted from dance music to screaming thrash crap. My hottie was snagged by a girl whose dress was cut so low she was showing nipple. I couldn't compete with that, so I limped off for something to drink. I waited in line, checking over my shoulder for Gilroy, got two cups of punch, and hurried back to our table.

Nat and I leaned our heads together and I gave her the whole story about how I wound up with the dress and how I snuck in. She cracked up when I told her that Grandma was the magic seamstress.

"That totally explains why she kept trying to fatten you up," Nat laughed. "She kept saying your butt needed to be bigger and that I needed to make you eat ice cream." She laughed again. "You are the only girl here who needed to gain weight for the prom."

"I wish she would have told me," I said. "I would have eaten more muffins."

The music was slow now and a little sucky, to be honest, but that gave us a chance to sit back and check out the rest of our class.

Most of the girls looked great, but when I looked closely I realized there were some skanks mixed in, dressed like rejects from a Britney Spears video. Everybody had kicked off their high heels. The basketball team was wearing shimmering halter dresses that showed off the muscles in their backs. A couple girls were wearing dresses that looked like they cost a thousand bucks. Others were definitely dressed à la Wal-Mart, but they were smiling just the same and looking every bit as pretty. The goth girls had matching protest flowers, droopy dandelions tucked into black rubber bands around their wrists. Their dresses looked like they were stolen out of a graveyard, but they matched their boots, so it was all good.

The men of Carceras really came through for their dates, got to give them that. Fifty different kinds of tuxedoes, top hats, vests, waistcoats with watch chains, shiny shoes, and sunglasses. Something about a tuxedo, I swear. They all looked respectable, responsible, and hot, with their chins up, their shoulders back, the creases on their pants sharp enough to cut paper. I definitely had to distribute the condoms before midnight.

Nat finished her punch and tapped my shoulder. "Get a load of that one." She pointed to Persia Faulkner, surrounded by her perfect popular posse, as usual. The rest of Carceras

looked good. Persia and her girls looked like honest-to-God rap divas. Their dresses fit better, their jewelry blinged brighter, and their asses jiggled tighter.

"They've been drinking Chivas all night," Nat said. "Only the best for the Queen Bitch."

"Come on," I said. "Cut her some slack. She's not as bad as you think."

"You're joking, right?"

"No, I'm serious. She helped make this happen, you know. She's been nice to me all week. Watch."

I got up and worked my way through the crowd to Persia. Nat was right. The whole group reeked of alcohol.

"Hey," I told her. "You look great."

The Persia Posse looked me over top to bottom and laughed at my slippers. Some people are so ignorant.

"I love your dress," I tried.

Persia blinked. "You talkin' to me?"

"I just wanted to see how the ride turned out for you guys and to say thanks for helping. You know, the tickets and everything. . . ."

"Who *are* you?" asked one of the Persia wannabes. The rest of them snickered like little dogs.

"I wasn't talking to you," I told her.

Persia leaned forward on her heels. "You're not talking to me neither. Get out my face."

The little dogs in their rhinestone chokers and press-on nails howled.

I limped back to the table.

"What'd she say?" Nat asked.

"She loves my dress," I said. "More punch?"

149.

The next two hours flew by. In between dancing with my girls, my guy friends, my friends who were guys, and a couple potential dates I gave my number to, I helped Nat deal with the behind-the-scenes crap.

Everybody who had a problem came to us. Some needed "official" action. Nat called security about the fight in the courtyard and the rumors of scumbags from a rival high school trying to plant smoke bombs in the boys' room. The little problems were easier: too much orange soda, not enough diet, a cake that wound up on the floor, complaints about the music, girls whose boobs kept popping out of their strapless dresses. We dealt with it all: a few phone calls and five cases of soda were delivered, the custodians cleaned up the cake in a flash, and the girls with the wandering boobs were told to keep their damn arms down—duh. Oh, and I personally yelled at the clueless ho going down on her date behind the bleachers. I mean *puh-leeze, have some dignity.*

The biggest problem was avoiding Gilroy. The girls let everybody know that he was trying to bust me and ruin my night. It wasn't that I was popular or anything, but everybody hated Gilroy so much they wanted to piss him off. So I had a couple hundred spies watching my back. I got used to having my arm pulled to drag me out of sight, or a big guy stepping in front of me, or a total stranger throwing her arms around

me to hide me from the vice principal of pain and torment.

The English teachers were way more awesome than I thought they'd be. First, they looked fine, for old people who don't earn much money. They cleaned up real good. Second, they were cool about not interfering with most of what happened on the dance floor and in the dark corners of the room. They let us act like normal teenagers, but didn't let anybody put on a porn show, know what I mean? In fact, it was that really hot teacher who told me about the ho blowing her boyfriend's mind under the bleachers. He thought it would be better if I broke it up than if he did—not so embarrassing for the girl. I didn't think anything could embarrass her, but it was sweet of him to think that.

The third cool English teacher thing was, they didn't narc on me to Gilroy. They didn't like him any better than we did.

One unplanned teacher showed up; our weird old Math sub. I ran into him when I was taking delivery of the diet soda at the loading dock.

"What are you doing here?" I asked.

"Trying to sneak in," he said. "I'm not sure how much longer I'll have a job around here. Gilroy's a real jerk."

"Tell me about it."

"Here, let me give you a hand." He loaded the soda cases onto the cart for me. "I promised some of your classmates I'd give them my business card. They're potential clients."

We pushed the cart towards the gym. "So you're here to get people thinking about insurance, is that it?"

"Exactly right, Miss Hannigan. You can never be too careful."

I thought about the cardboard box of you-know-whats hiding under the table. "I have something you could hand out with your card. Trust me, people will remember you. They'll thank you, too. My generation believes in insurance."

150.

After I turned over the condoms to the Math sub, I saw Gilroy headed my way. I hurried over to the photography corner to hide. The photographer had set up with his digital camera and big lights, taking pictures of couples for a little cash. I stood behind the background curtain until I got the signal that Gilroy was gone.

The music stopped. "Okay, okay, okay," the DJ said. "I need everybody to clear the dance floor please, except for, ah," he checked a piece of paper in front of him, "Charles Fournier and Junie Yoo."

"Here." The photographer passed out disposable cameras to me and the other kids standing near him. "I heard this was going to happen. Use these for candid shots. Give them back to me at the end of the night."

Yeah, Charles did it. In front of everybody, girls squealing, guys rolling their eyes, Junie shaking like the first leaf that falls in October, Charles suddenly looking ten years old, he got down on one knee in the middle of the dance floor, and pulled out a ring with an itty-bitty diamond chip in it.

"Will you marry me?" he asked, his voice cracking.

I think Junie said "Yes." It was hard to tell because she was crying so hard. Camera flashes exploded all over the gym, and

a wave of girls with stupid ideas about rings with itty-bitty diamonds in them crashed onto the dance floor. I wanted to raise my hand and say "Excuse me, don't you think you're a little young, you still watch Cartoon Network," but then Gilroy popped up again, so I ducked out into the back hall.

151.

"There you are, missy." It wasn't Gilroy, thank God. It was the head custodian. "You got a problem."

"I took care of the soda that we ordered," I said. "And I locked up the loading gate like you said."

"I thought we had a deal," he growled.

"We did," I said. "We do. Are you talking about the money? Nat will pay you at the end of the night."

"You break the deal and we walk off the job. We walk off the job and old Gilroy will shut down this dance."

"It's not a dance, it's a prom. What are you talking about?"

I couldn't believe it. There I was, having the best night of my life, and a guy with a push broom was shaking me down.

In the twinkling lights he looked like a tired, disappointed owl. "Follow me."

We walked out the back door of the gym towards the locker room hall. I kept close to him with my head down. The custodian went into the girls' locker room with me right behind. He took me past the lockers, past the coaches' office, to the bathroom door.

He opened it.

The smell hit me like a slap in the face.

Oh, no. Not tonight. Not in this beautiful dress, please God, I'm begging.

The custodian leaned towards me, his eyes bigger than ever. "Our deal was no vomit clean-up. A deal's a deal."

He turned and walked out, sweeping as he went. I took a deep breath and stepped inside.

The smell and the sound were unmistakable.

Persia Faulkner was on her knees worshipping the porcelain god. In the stalls on either side of her were two of her wannabe friends. All three of them were puking their guts and their Chivas Regal out.

And I had a camera in my hand.

How could I resist?

I shot the entire roll of film, group shots and close-ups. Then I had my own deal for Persia and her girls.

"Clean up this mess and I'll give these pictures and negatives to you on Monday. Screw up and I share them with the whole school."

I was good.

152.

I went straight to the dance floor and joined in. We were all shaking it, spinning, sexing, slinking, shouting out, raising the roof and bringing down the house. There was love on the dance floor: Monica and Mark; Leeann and Big Mike; Quong and Danny; Dalinda and Ian; Junie and Charles; and Lauren, Aisha, Nat, and me.

The whole committee danced around Nat's wheelchair,

and then the songs came faster and faster, and the heat turned up, and we were moving, moving to a beat never heard before in the halls of Carceras High School, arms waving, hips popping, hearts locked into the same rhythm, the same beat, until we danced so hard I thought for sure we were going to float all the way to heaven.

153.

Everything was perfect right up to the minute the cops arrested me.

154.

By the time I stood in front of the night court judge, it was almost morning.

The officers had been real nice to me, because I wasn't drunk or high or a bitch. The tall one who found me a jacket when I got cold said he felt bad about the whole thing, but somebody from the school had pressured the chief of police so they didn't have a choice. He told me he had been named the king of his prom, out in Denver, but that his date left with his best friend, so the night had been a bummer. He hoped I had a better time.

I said I did.

Natalia's dad called around, and I wound up being defended by another Russian. We have a lot of them where we live.

Ma showed up, too. She waved at the judge when he walked in. Turns out they went to high school together, and the judge's sister had been on the softball team with Ma and

Aunt Linny. The judge couldn't stand Gilroy's Social Studies class, either.

He dismissed the charges and told me my dress was very pretty.

155.

Mr. Shulmensky drove us home just as the sun came up over New Jersey. We got to the top of a hill and had to stop at a Wawa so Ma could use the bathroom. No way was she gonna make it home, she said. Mr. Shulmensky said no problem, he wanted to get a newspaper and a cup of coffee anyway.

I got out and leaned against the car. There were a few clouds in the sky. Maybe they had been partying all night, too. Out in the west, towards Pittsburgh, the moon was setting, pulling a couple stars down with it. I liked how it was all happening at once, the moon and stars pinking up in the sunrise, the whole world spinning around like it was supposed to.

156.

Once upon a time there was a girl who got a life.

157.

Me.

How It All Turned Out

158.

Getting back to regular school after the prom was what you call extremely, horribly, ass-kicking hard, but I did it. Everybody did. We showed up to our classes, all us normal kids who for a couple hours had been masters of our universe. We woke up when the alarm rang, put on clean clothes and brushed our teeth, and walked through the Carceras metal detectors for all those last days in May and June. We studied for finals, most of us, and dragged our butts to class and took the tests. We passed.

I passed.

Nat got an awesome financial aid package from Temple,

and a bunch of scholarships. She only has to take out a little loan, so when she gets her college degree, she won't be killed with payments for forty years. She decided to stay home and take the city bus down Broad Street to Temple. That's one of the coolest things about living so close to Philly. The bus will take you anywhere.

As we got ready for graduation, the flowers in Nat's grandmother's garden bloomed like nobody's business. That old lady definitely had weird juju stuff in her fingers, crazy Russian magic or something. The roses were as red as fresh blood and as fat as a fist. I didn't know the names of the other flowers, but Ma did. She'd sit in a lawn chair next to the fence with her feet propped up on a tricycle or laundry basket and watch those flowers grow, fifty shades of pink and yellow and purple. Her belly kept growing, too. We had a pool going on the size of the baby. If I won, Ma was going to be in the Guinness record book, for sure.

The weekend that Nat and Mr. S. moved Grandma into the nursing home, Ma cut all the flowers. I helped her arrange them in vases and plastic buckets, then we drove to the nursing home and filled Grandma's room with color. Then I drove Ma to the hospital at twice the legal speed limit.

My little sister, Adrian, was born in the entrance to the emergency room.

159.

It was Adrian who helped me figure everything out.

Ma was on the stretcher talking about birth control to the

banged-up thugs who had just watched her give birth. The doctor checked out Adrian, wrapped her up, and handed her to me. I only had her for a second; you know how hospital people are. But it was the longest second of my life. Hers, too, I'm sure.

She looked like a prize fighter; kind of bloody, a bit confused, eyes swollen and blinking. I cleaned off her face with a corner of the blanket. She reminded me of me: a little on the scrawny side, red hair, pale skin, and blue eyes.

Those eyes opened wider. She looked right at me.

Wow.

I decided to move out of my parents' house.

Talk about a sucker punch. It hit me like a left hook out of nowhere that moving down to the basement would totally suck, and moving into a rat hole with someone like TJ would suck even more, and I had to find another way out of there, but I didn't want to go too far, because this little girl needed me to show her the ropes and all.

When they took Adrian out of my arms, she cried.

That was cool.

160.

So we got through all the hospital stuff, and Ma and Ade came home. We had a combo graduation and new baby party and saved a ton of money on food and drinks. Ade was a hit at the party. She peed up a storm and wailed loud enough to be heard over the music, which was good.

I sprung my big idea on Nat and her dad the first time I

took Adrian to visit Grandma Shulmensky. They were cool with it. So was my dad. Ma took a little extra convincing, but Aunt Linny pointed out that I'd be close, and Aunt Sharon said it meant I could babysit for Adrian when Barry Manilow came to town, and Aunt Joan told Ma to shut up and let me have a life.

TJ, well he tried. He sent me cards, he sent me beer. He came around to my graduation party with roses, but it was over, dead and gone. Don't know why I stayed with him so long. What a waste. I heard that he moved some chick from Cherry Hill into the slimeball apartment, and I'm just counting the days before she turns up pregnant or he gets his first felony conviction or both. I never did find out the name of his sister's baby.

It's a little weird now, paying rent to Mr. Shulmensky and living down the hall from Nattie, who always leaves a mess in the bathroom. I don't care if that cast is still on her leg, how hard is it to hang up your towel? And to be honest, I'm nervous about this whole community college thing, though Nat keeps telling me it'll be way better than high school, 'cause I'm in charge of me, and if I don't like it, I can always quit, which no way I'm gonna do, because I'm paying for all of it, and you'd better believe I'm gonna get my money's worth.

I'm taking Liberal Arts classes for now. It doesn't mean, like, drawing or painting kind of art, or being a liberal like in politics, which is what I thought the first time I heard it. It means I want to learn a few things before I decide what I want to be. It's too bad they don't give degrees in prom manage-

ment. Accounting sounds kind of interesting, because at least when numbers don't add up right, you can figure out where you went wrong. I even thought about maybe becoming a teacher's aide, or even a teacher some day. I know a few things about normal kids.

Hell, I could write a book about them.

ACKNOWLEDGMENTS

Many, many, many thanks to the members of my personal Prom Court who stood behind the creation of this book—

Prom Queens

Stephanie and Meredith Anderson, for letting me take over the couch and for keeping me supplied with popcorn.

Jessica Larrabee, for being so patient with me.

Sharyn November and Regina Hayes, for constant cheerleading and support.

The women of the Bucks County Children's Writers Group, for riding the roller coaster with me.

Amy Berkower and the staff at Writers House, for taking care of business.

Sarah Henry, for saving my sanity.

Prom Kings

Christian Larrabee, for letting me write during that awesome blizzard.

Scot Larrabee, my husband, for absolutely everything.

Special Mention

A loud, rowdy shout-out to all the "normal" kids who talked to me the last couple of years and told me nobody ever writes about them. Hope you like it.

The Music

This book was written to the tunes of Beethoven, Bruce Springsteen, Coldplay, Eminem, Norah Jones, and Sting. And, of course, the tunes of Y100 in Philadelphia.

LAURIE HALSE ANDERSON is the author of the award-winning novels *Speak*, *Fever 1793*, and *Catalyst*, as well as five picture books. The night of *her* senior prom, she was shoveling manure on a pig farm in Denmark. She lives with her family in Central New York.

Visit her Web site at **www.writerlady.com**.

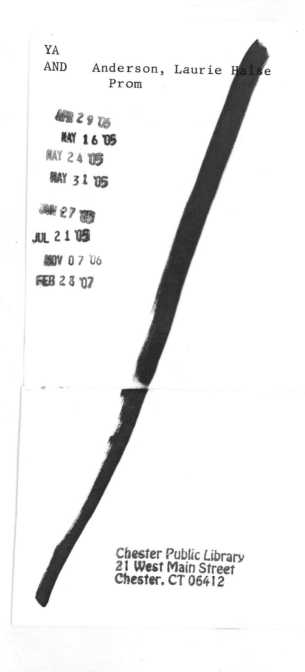

Novels by
LAURIE HALSE ANDERSON

SPEAK

FEVER 1793

CATALYST

PROM

Prom

DATE DUE

JUL 07 '09			
MAY 2 9 '09			
AUG 20 '09			
JUN 1 5 '10			
MAR 1 1 '11			
APR 26 '11			
JUN 16 '11			
JUL 06 '11			
JUN 07 '12			
JUL 1 3 '12			
SEP 2 0 '12			
AP 2 5 '13			
SE 0 6 '13			
OC 1 0 '16			

Demco, Inc. 38-293

Book 📚🐻📚 Buddies

Marco Polo
Brave Explorer

Meet the Book Buddies, toys that can
be checked out from the library,
just like books. For the Book Buddies,
every borrowing is a new adventure!

Look for the next installment
in the Book Buddies series,
coming Spring 2022!

CYNTHIA LORD is the author of award-winning middle-grade fiction titles such as the Newbery Honor Book *Rules*, *Touch Blue*, *Half a Chance*, *A Handful of Stars*, and *Because of the Rabbit*. She is also the author of the Hot Rod Hamster picture book and early reader series as well as the Shelter Pet Squad chapter book series. Cynthia Lord lives in Maine.

STEPHANIE GRAEGIN is the author-illustrator of *Little Fox in the Forest* and the illustrator of many other picture books, including *You Were the First* by Patricia MacLachlan and *Water in the Park* by Emily Jenkins. Stephanie Graegin lives in Brooklyn.